TINA
THE TIGER

WRITTEN BY JOHN STORMS
ILLUSTRATED BY ROBERT STORMS

HEIAN

© 1994 Text by John Storms
Illustrations by Robert Storms

ISBN: 0-89346-814-2

Heian International
1815 W. 205th St. Suite.# 301
Torrance, CA 90501

First printing 1995

95 96 97 98 99 10 9 8 7 6 5 4 3 2 1

Printed in Singapore

Hi! My name is Tina, and I'm a Bengal tiger.

I live in the high grasslands and jungles of India. Tigers also live in some remote parts of Asia, from the snowy forests of Siberia to the bamboo forests and mangrove swamps of Malaysia.

We can live almost anywhere, as long as we have three things. We need bushes and trees to hide in while we hunt; animals to catch for our food; and shade and water to cool us on hot days.

2

Our favorite food is meat. I can eat up to fifty pounds of meat in one meal! Of course, when I do eat that much, I end up burping for a week! **BURP!** Excuse me! When possible, tigers prefer to eat large animals like wild boar, antelope and buffalo.

Sometimes, however, we can only find small animals like frogs or turtles or fish. I hate catching frogs! They all start jumping around and pretty soon I'm so cross-eyed that I can't even catch <u>one</u>!

4

When I can't even find small animals, I get so hungry that I'll eat anything--even *GRASS!* **YUK**! I hate eating grass! It makes me feel like a big striped cow! Then everyone laughs at me, even Carl the cobra, and he never laughs at anything!

5

I eat many different foods and I bet you'll never guess which is my favorite. It's porcupines! Unfortunately, catching a porcupine can be very painful. When it sees me, it runs as fast as it can--*BACKWARDS*--and tries to stab me with its long sharp quills! **YEOW!** That hurts! Maybe I should try to find a new favorite food--one without quills!

Tigers are the largest cats in the world, and we need a lot of food. That's why we spend so much of our time hunting. We don't hunt in groups like lions or wolves. Instead, each tiger hunts alone, usually at night.

Can you guess how I find animals in the dark? *Nooo*, I don't use a flashlight. I don't need one because my eyes can see in the dark. But for hunting, I prefer to use my ears. I rotate my ears around like little radar dishes. Then I can hear even the quietest animals moving around in the dark.

Of course, I have to be very quiet too. If the animals hear me, they will immediately run away. When I'm hunting, I sneak silently through the brush, hiding behind trees and bushes, in order to get as close as possible to the animals.

Then--I leap out and **ROAR!** If I'm lucky I catch my dinner, but most of the time all of the animals get away. I'm not very fast and I get tired quickly so if I don't catch anything on my jump--there's no dinner for me!

My feet are also a problem. I have very soft pads on the bottom of my feet which help me walk quietly through the jungle. But if I chase an animal over rough, stony ground, the stones and rocks really hurt my soft feet. Pretty soon I'm lying down, holding my feet and crying: **OUCH! OUCH! OUCH!**

However, my biggest hunting problem isn't my soft feet or my slow running. It's those "tattle-tale" birds and monkeys up in the trees! They love to sit right above my head and tell everyone where I am! I can't sneak up on anything with all their pointing and screaming!

After a long night of hunting, I'm ready for a cool drink of water. When its hot, I don't just get a drink, I lie right down in the water. *Ahhh* --that feels good! Sometimes I even go swimming. What? You thought all cats hated water? Not tigers--we **love** it!

The only thing I don't like about swimming is getting my face wet. Getting water up your nose is no fun! AH-CHOO! No fun at all! That's why I always back into the water tail first. That keeps my face nice and dry.

On hot summer days I like to go swimming with my friend, Timmy. He usually wins all of our swimming races.

But when we have jumping contests, it's my turn to win. One day, I jumped across a river that was over twenty feet wide, and I didn't get a single drop of water on me! Even the birds and monkeys cheered for me that day!

Another of our favorite games is hide-and-go-seek. Nobody hides in tall grass better than Timmy. Say--maybe you could come and help me find him. Later, we could all go swimming. But remember, <u>do not</u> splash water in my face!

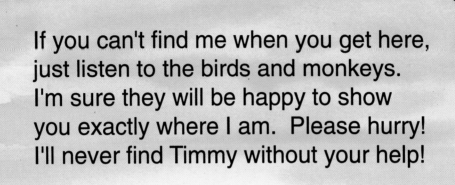

If you can't find me when you get here,
just listen to the birds and monkeys.
I'm sure they will be happy to show
you exactly where I am. Please hurry!
I'll never find Timmy without your help!